DISNEY · PIXAR

Adapted by
Courtney Carbone

Illustrated by
Francesca Risoldi

Designed by
Tony Fejeran

A GOLDEN BOOK • NEW YORK

Copyright © 2021 Disney Enterprises, Inc. and Pixar. Vespa is a trademark of Piaggio & C. S.p.A.
All rights reserved. Published in the United States by Golden Books, an imprint of Random House Children's Books,
a division of Penguin Random House LLC, 1745 Broadway, New York, NY 10019, and in Canada by Penguin Random House
Canada Limited, Toronto, in conjunction with Disney Enterprises, Inc. Golden Books, A Golden Book,
A Little Golden Book, the G colophon, and the distinctive gold spine are registered trademarks of Penguin Random House LLC.
rhcbooks.com
ISBN 978-0-7364-4193-3 (trade) — ISBN 978-0-7364-4194-0 (ebook)
Printed in the United States of America
10 9 8 7 6 5 4 3

Luca was a friendly sea monster who lived with his family in the ocean. He spent his days herding a flock of goatfish.

Though he dreamed about life above the surface, Luca was **forbidden to go on land.** His parents warned him that humans were dangerous.

One day, Luca met Alberto, another young sea
monster. As Alberto collected some new treasures,
he accidentally took Luca's shepherding crook.
Luca chased him all the way to the surface!

When they reached land, Luca and Alberto
transformed into humans! Everything around
Luca was strange but amazing.

Then Alberto took Luca to his **hideout.** It was full of neat human things, including a poster of a shiny **Vespa.** Luca was fascinated.

Looking around, he realized they could **build their own Vespa!** The boys got to work right away.

Every day on the island, Luca and Alberto made all
kinds of Vespas with anything they could find. They
even rode one together and **soared through the air!**
Luca had never had so much fun.

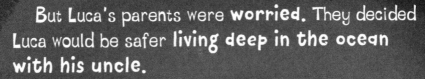

But Luca's parents were **worried.** They decided Luca would be safer **living deep in the ocean with his uncle.**

Before they could send him away, Luca left to find Alberto.

Luca and Alberto swam to the seaside town of
Portorosso, where they met a human girl named **Giulia**.
    She was unsure about the boys at first, but she soon
realized that they would be perfect teammates for a
local race called the **Portorosso Cup**. With the prize
money, they could buy a real **Vespa**—and then
they could go anywhere!

The boys met Giulia's dad, Massimo, who was a
fisherman. They agreed to work for him in exchange for
the race's entry fee. Massimo's cat, Machiavelli, kept
a close eye on the boys. He smelled something fishy!

Luca and Alberto knew that winning wasn't going to be easy. **Ercole**, the five-time race champion, was also competing. The bully **taunted the three friends** and vowed to defeat them.

More determined than ever, the team began training for the **three events** of the Portorosso Cup.

Giulia practiced swimming.

Alberto practiced eating pasta.

And Luca practiced riding a bike.

Over time, they became good friends.
Giulia and Luca loved to read and learn.

Luca was amazed that Giulia went to school.
He wanted to go, too!

Alberto began to feel left out. He didn't want Luca to go to school with Giulia, so he revealed that he was a sea monster! **Giulia was shocked**, but Luca stayed quiet.

Hearing the commotion, Ercole ran up and **threw his harpoon.** Alberto escaped just in time.

Giulia soon figured out that Luca was a sea monster, too. She was worried that Luca would be in danger if anyone knew the truth about him.

Later, Luca found Alberto. He was angry at Luca and didn't want to race anymore. But Luca wouldn't give up. He promised to get them a Vespa.

Finally, the day of the Portorosso Cup arrived. Luca decided to race alone to protect Giulia. It was risky to hide his sea monster identity.

During the first event, he wore a **diving suit** to avoid transforming in the water.

Next, he **completed** the pasta-eating competition.

During the bike race, Luca **zoomed ahead**, passing racers left and right.

He ran into his parents, who had been searching for him. But Luca kept pedaling as hard as he could.

It began to rain. Alberto arrived to help Luca, but he got into trouble: the rain transformed him into a sea monster! A crowd trapped Alberto in a net.

Luca rode into the rain and **rescued his friend.**
Now everyone knew **Luca** was a sea monster, too! The
boys raced away as **Ercole** chased them.

Before Ercole could take aim with his harpoon, Giulia **crashed her bike** into him!

Seeing their injured friend, Luca and Alberto came to a screeching halt. They climbed off their bike and rushed to Giulia's side.

Luca and Alberto were nervous as the crowd watched them. Massimo was the first to step forward. To everyone's surprise, he **accepted the boys** as they were. And he pointed out something important: Luca and Alberto had stopped their bike just past the finish line. **They had won the race!**

Later that evening, Luca and Alberto finally
bought their very own Vespa, and the group
gathered in Massimo's backyard to share a meal.
Luca's family was **welcomed with open arms.**

It was soon time for Giulia to go away to school.
But she wasn't the only one. As a surprise, Alberto had
talked to Luca's parents, sold the Vespa, and bought a
train ticket. Luca would be going to school!

Luca wanted his friend to come with him, but
Alberto planned to stay in Portorosso with Massimo.
Even if they were apart, they knew their
summer memories—and their **friendship**—
would last forever.